THE KARGIL DIVAS COLOR

3 MAY 1999

MR VIVEK KUMAR PANDEY

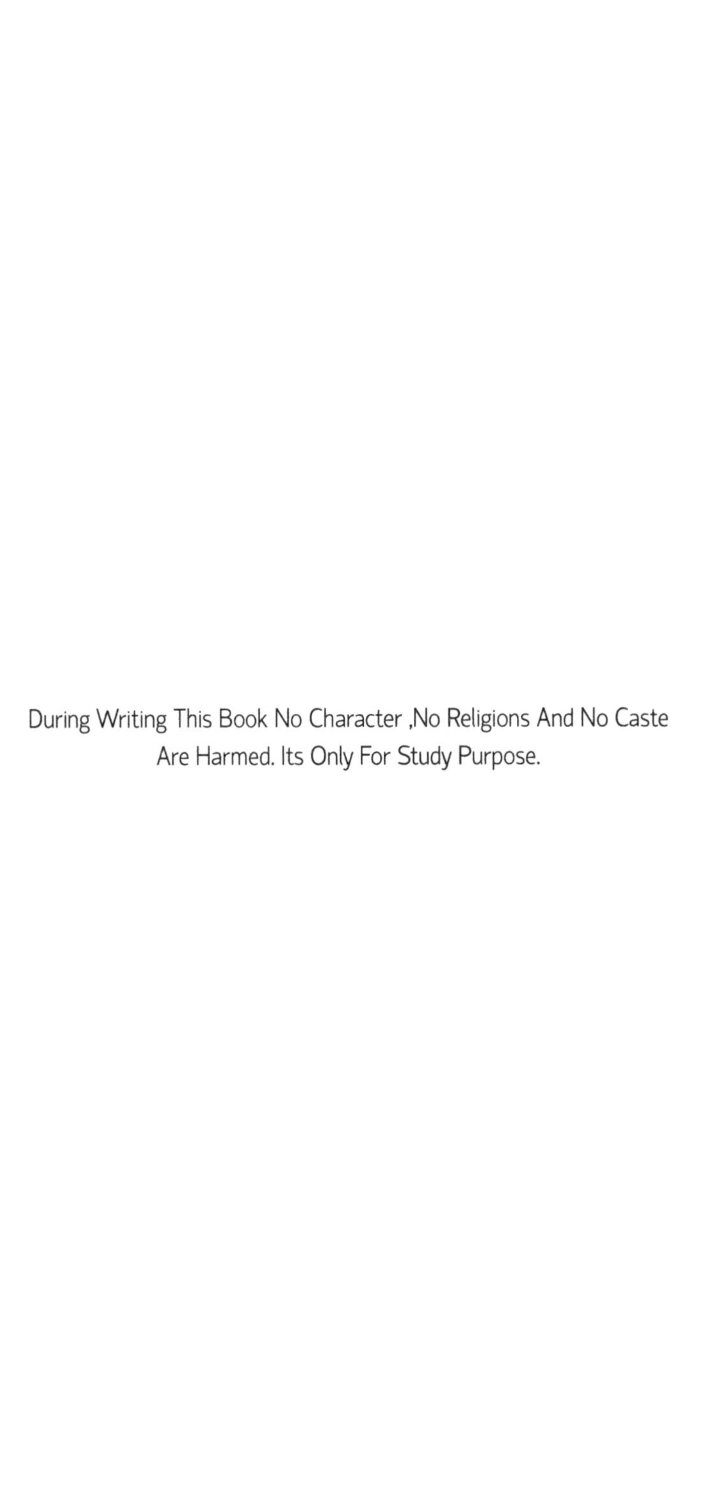

During Writing This Book No Character ,No Religions And No Caste Are Harmed. Its Only For Study Purpose.

Contents

Foreword

We should be proud. Kargil war is such a victory story, which is considered as an example. You all have to know what happened during the war, how many soldiers were killed. During Writing This Book No Character, No Religion & No Caste Are Harmed.It's only for study purpose written by Mr Vivek Kumar Pandey. This Book Fully Color Editions.

Preface

Author biography in English :MY NAME IS VIVEK KUMAR PANDEY . I WAS BORN IN 30 SEP 2002,I AM FROM SURAT GUJARAT INDIA.MY DREAM WAS TO BE GOOD WRITERS ,MY FAMILY SUPPORTED ME TO SUCCESSFUL AND I CAN DO IT MY SELF.How do I write? That is a question, I believe, that can be honestly answered by me."CELEBRATING YOUNGEST WRITER AWARD WINNER IN GUJARAT 1ST RANK" MR PANDEY JI . I may think I did a good job writing something. The reader is the one who decides the quality of my writing. I do find writing to be natural to me and therefore find it to be a real challenge. My trick as a challenged writer is to do the best I can and know that I am happy with the final outcome. It may take a while to do my best and there may be quite a few problems I run into along the way.

I am not a greedy person those who are thinking about me and my self I never tried it anyone people suffering from sadness ,I trying to get promoted people suffering from happincss and joy in your LIfe Time. Now in current situation in India and also world people are unemployed and have no many but our indian governor help to people to get free food from ration card , i also take part in leadership team ,i am Motivational spcakcr , Film script writer. There was my two dream firstly writer and secondly actor & also my own film is upcoming soon i done almost completely completed script for my film .I AM GOING TO SAY WORD OF HEART TOUCH OUT PLEASE READ IT" , firstly i thanks my father he supports me in this field they always getting inspired me by own his words and behavior ,they always said that he was a biggest person in the world in future and also they purchase fruit and chocolate for me in anytime & anyway , firstly my father buy him then call me Vivek you want a chocolate i will say yes papa but how many tell me ,papa: you tell me how much i buy him i told 1 or 2 chocolate but my father purchase whole the boxes of chocolate and they get suprised me. MY FATHER WAS BORN IN " 20 SEPTEMBER" 1971 IN INDIA.

1) MY FATHER FAVORITE CLOTHES IS KURTA PAIJMA AND ALSO STYLES SHOE

2) FAVORITE SINGER IS KISHORE DA

3) FAVORITE STATE GUJARAT AND KOLKATA , HIS VILLAGE IN BIHAR

4) FAVORITE COLOR BLACK AND WHITE

THEY ALSO LOVE cricket like IPL and one day t-20 .they also like watching a News daily and heard the song daily ,they also interested in tik tok video but in current time tik tok is banned in india but also few videos are in you tube. In lockdown time my family and me very enjoy day daily. my father play daily ludo with his sister and son, daughter.they always loved tea and coffee anytime call me "I. I make it tea for my father but some reason after the April to june they are suffering from fever and cough , weakness on 6 June 2020 my father death. they not told me say bye bye his life. After death of 6 June on 10 june my mom and dad anniversary.but my father is Best in the world they can do anything for me please take care of father and respect it of your parents.

CHAPTER ONE

The Kargil Divas Color

- **Kargil War Date3 May – 26 July 1999**

During Writing This Book No Character ,No Religions And No Caste Are Harmed. Its Only For Study Purpose.

The Kargil War, also known as the Kargil conflict,was fought between India and Pakistan from May to July 1999 in the Kargil district of Jammu and Kashmir and elsewhere along the Line of Control (LoC). In India, the conflict is also referred to as Operation Vijay 'Victory'), which was the codename of the Indian military operation in the region. The role of the Indian Air Force in acting jointly with the Indian Army was aimed at flushing out both the Pakistan Army and irregular Pakistani troops from vacated Indian positions along the LoC, in what was designated as Operation Safed Sagar ('White Sea').

The conflict was triggered by the infiltration of Pakistani troops—disguised as Kashmiri militants—into strategic positions on the Indian side of the LoC, which serves as the de facto border between the two countries in the disputed region of Kashmir. During its initial stages, Pakistan blamed the fighting entirely on independent Kashmiri insurgents, but documents left behind by casualties and later statements by Pakistan's Prime Minister and Chief of Army Staff showed the involvement of Pakistani paramilitary forces, led by General Ashraf Rashid. The Indian Army, later supported by the Indian Air Force, recaptured a majority of the positions on the Indian side of the LoC; facing international diplomatic opposition, Pakistani forces withdrew from all remaining Indian positions along the LoC.

The Kargil War is the most recent example of high-altitude warfare in mountainous terrain, and as such, posed significant logistical problems for the combatting sides. It also marks one of only two instances of conventional warfare between nuclear-armed states (alongside the Sino-Soviet border conflict). India had conducted its first successful test in 1974; Pakistan, which had been developing its nuclear capability in secret since around the same time, conducted its first known tests in 1998, just two weeks after a second series of tests by India.

Before the Partition of India in 1947, Kargil was a tehsil of Ladakh, a sparsely populated region with diverse linguistic, ethnic and religious groups, living in isolated valleys separated by some of the world's highest mountains. The Indo-Pakistani War of 1947-1948 concluded with the Line of Control bisecting the Ladakh district, with the Skardu tehsil going to Pakistan (now part of Gilgit-Baltistan).After Pakistan's defeat in the Indo-Pakistani War of 1971, the two nations signed the Simla Agreement promising not to engage in armed conflict with respect to that boundary.

The town of Kargil is located 205 km (127 mi) from Srinagar, facing the Northern Areas across the LOC. Like other areas in the Himalayas, Kargil has a continental climate. Summers are cool with frigid nights, while winters are long and chilly with temperatures often dropping to −48 °C (−54 °F).

An Indian national highway (NH 1) connecting Srinagar to Leh cuts through Kargil. The area that witnessed the infiltration and fighting is a 160-kilometre (100 mi) long stretch of ridges overlooking this only road linking Srinagar and Leh. The military outposts on the ridges above the highway were generally around 5,000 m (16,000 ft) high, with a few as high as 5,485 m (17,995 ft). Apart from the district capital, Kargil, the populated areas near the front line in the conflict included the Mushkoh Valley and the town of Drass, southwest of Kargil, as well as the Batalik sector and other areas northeast of Kargil.

Kargil was targeted partly because the terrain was conducive to the preemptive seizure of several unoccupied military positions. With tactically vital features and well-prepared defensive posts atop the peaks, a defender on the high ground would enjoy advantages akin to that of a fortress. Any attack to dislodge a defender from high ground in mountain warfare requires a far higher ratio of attackers to defenders, and the difficulties would be exacerbated by the high altitude and freezing temperatures.

Kargil is just 173 km (107 mi) from the Pakistani-controlled town of Skardu, which was capable of providing logistical and artillery support to Pakistani combatants. A road between Kargil and Skardu exists, which was closed in 1949.

- The town of Kargil is strategically located

After the Indo-Pakistani War of 1971, there had been a long period with relatively few direct armed conflicts involving the military forces of the two neighbours—notwithstanding the efforts of both nations to control the Siachen Glacier by establishing military outposts on the surrounding mountains ridges and the resulting military skirmishes in the 1980s. During the 1990s, however, escalating tensions and conflict due to separatist activities in Kashmir, some of which were supported by Pakistan, as well as the conducting of nuclear tests by both countries in 1998, led to an increasingly belligerent atmosphere. In an attempt to defuse the situation, both countries signed the Lahore Declaration in February 1999, promising to provide a peaceful and bilateral solution to the Kashmir conflict.

During the winter of 1998–1999, some elements of the Pakistani Armed Forces were covertly training and sending Pakistani troops and paramilitary forces, some allegedly in the guise of mujahideen, into territory on the Indian side of the LOC. The infiltration was codenamed "Operation Badr" its aim was to sever the link between Kashmir and Ladakh, and cause Indian forces to withdraw from the Siachen Glacier, thus forcing India to negotiate a settlement of the broader Kashmir dispute. Pakistan also believed that any tension in the region would internationalise the Kashmir issue, helping it to secure a speedy resolution. Yet another goal may have been to boost the morale of the decade-long rebellion in Jammu and Kashmir by taking a proactive role.

Pakistani Lieutenant General Shahid Aziz, and then head of ISI analysis wing, has confirmed there were no mujahideen but only regular Pakistan Army soldiers who took part in the Kargil War. "There were no Mujahideen, only taped wireless messages, which fooled no one. Our soldiers were made to occupy barren ridges, with hand held weapons and ammunition", Lt Gen Aziz wrote in his article in The Nation daily in January 2013.

Some writers have speculated that the operation's objective may also have been retaliation for India's Operation Meghdoot in 1984 that seized much of Siachen Glacier.

According to India's then army chief Ved Prakash Malik, and many scholars, much of the background planning, including construction of logistical supply routes, had been undertaken much earlier. On several occasions during the 1980s and 1990s, the army had given Pakistani leaders (Zia ul Haq and Benazir Bhutto) similar proposals for infiltration into the Kargil region, but the plans had been shelved for fear of drawing the nations into all-out war.

Some analysts believe that the blueprint of attack was reactivated soon after Pervez Musharraf was appointed chief of army staff in October 1998. After the war, Nawaz Sharif, Prime Minister of Pakistan during the Kargil conflict, claimed that he was unaware of the plans, and that he first learned about the situation when he received an urgent phone call from Atal Bihari Vajpayee, his counterpart in India.Sharif attributed the plan to Musharraf and "just two or three of his cronies", a view shared by some Pakistani writers who have stated that only four generals, including Musharraf, knew of the plan. Musharraf, however, asserted that Sharif had been briefed on the Kargil operation 15 days ahead of Vajpayee's journey to Lahore on 20 February.

- Kargil order of battle

Date (1999)Event

1. 3 MayA Pakistani intrusion in the Kargil district is reported by local shepherds.

2. 5 MayIndian Army patrols are sent out in response to earlier reports; 5 Indian soldiers are captured and subsequently killed.
3. 9 MayHeavy shelling by the Pakistan Army damages Indian ammunition dumps in Kargil.
4. 10 MayMultiple infiltrations across the LoC are confirmed in Dras, Kaksar, and Mushkoh sectors.
5. Mid-MayIndia moves in more soldiers from the Kashmir Valley to Kargil district.
6. 26 MayThe Indian Air Force (IAF) begins airstrikes against suspected infiltrator positions.
7. 27 MayOne IAF MiG-21 and one MiG-27 aircraft are shot down by Anza surface-to-air missiles of the Pakistan Army's Air Defence Corps Flt. Lt. Kambampati Nachiketa (pilot of the MiG-27) is captured by a Pakistani patrol and given POW status (released on 3 June 1999).
8. 28 MayOne IAF Mi-17 is shot down by Pakistani forces; four crew members are killed.
9. 1 JuneThe Pakistan Army begins shelling operations on India's National Highway 1 in Kashmir and Ladakh.
10. 5 JuneIndia releases documents recovered from three Pakistani soldiers that officially indicate Pakistan's involvement in the conflict.
11. 6 JuneThe Indian Army begins a major offensive in Kargil.
12. 9 JuneIndian troops re-capture two key positions in the Batalik sector.
13. 11 JuneIndia releases intercepts of conversations between Pakistani COAS Gen. Pervez Musharraf (on a visit to China) and CGS Lt. Gen. Aziz Khan (in Rawalpindi) as proof of the Pakistan Army's involvement in the infiltrations.

14. 13 JuneIndian forces secure Tololing in Dras after a fierce battle with militias backed by Pakistani troops.
15. 15 JuneUnited States President Bill Clinton forces then Prime Minister of Pakistan, Nawaz Sharif to immediately pull all Pakistani troops and irregulars out from Kargil.
16. 29 JuneUnder pressure from the federal government, Pakistani forces begin their retreat from Indian-administered Kashmir and the Indian Army advances towards Tiger Hill.
17. 4 JulyThree Indian regiments (Sikh, Grenadiers and Naga) engage elements of the remaining Pakistani Northern Light Infantry regiment in the Battle of Tiger Hill. The region is recaptured by Indian forces after more than 12 hours of fighting.
18. 5 JulyPakistani Prime Minister Nawaz Sharif officially announces the Pakistan Army's withdrawal from Kargil following a meeting with POTUS Bill Clinton. Indian forces subsequently take control of Dras.
19. 7 JulyIndian troops recapture Jubar Heights in Batalik.
20. 11 JulyPakistani forces disengage from the region; India retakes key peak points in Batalik.
21. 14 JulyPrime Minister of India Atal Bihari Vajpayee declares Operation Vijay a success. The Indian government sets conditions for talks with Pakistan.
22. 26 JulyKargil War officially comes to an end. Indian Army announces the complete withdrawal of Pakistani irregular and regular forces.

There were three major phases to the Kargil War. First, Pakistan infiltrated forces into the Indian-controlled section of Kashmir and occupied strategic locations enabling it to bring NH1 within range of its artillery fire.

The next stage consisted of India discovering the infiltration and mobilising forces to respond to it. The final stage involved major battles by Indian and Pakistani forces resulting in India recapturing most of the territories held by Pakistani forces and the subsequent withdrawal of Pakistani forces back across the LOC after international pressure.

- Infiltration and military build-up

During February 1999, the Pakistan Army sent forces to occupy some posts on the Indian side of the LOC. Troops from the elite Special Services Group as well as four to seven battalions of the Northern Light Infantry (a paramilitary regiment not part of the regular Pakistani army at that time) covertly and overtly set up bases on 132 vantage points of the Indian-controlled region. According to some reports, these Pakistani forces were backed by Kashmiri guerrillas and Afghan mercenaries. According to General Ved Malik, the bulk of the infiltration occurred in April.

Pakistani intrusions took place in the heights of the lower Mushkoh Valley, along the Marpo La ridgeline in Dras, in Kaksar near Kargil, in the Batalik sector east of the Indus River, on the heights above of the Chorbat La sector where the LOC turns North and in the Turtuk sector south of the Siachen area.

- India discovers infiltration and mobilises

Initially, these incursions were not detected for a number of reasons: Indian patrols were not sent into some of the areas infiltrated by the Pakistani forces and heavy artillery fire by Pakistan in some areas provided cover for the infiltrators. But by the second week of May, the ambushing of an Indian patrol team led by Capt Saurabh Kalia, who acted on a tip-off by a local shepherd in the Batalik sector, led to the exposure of the infiltration. Initially, with little knowledge of the nature or extent of the infiltration, the Indian troops in the area assumed that the infiltrators were jihadis and claimed that they would evict them within a few days. Subsequent discovery of infiltration elsewhere along the LOC, and the difference in tactics employed by the infiltrators, caused the Indian army to realise that the plan of attack was on a much bigger scale. The total area seized by the ingress is generally accepted to between 130 and 200 km2 (50 and 80 sq mi).

The Government of India responded with Operation Vijay, a mobilisation of 200,000 Indian troops. However, because of the nature of the terrain, division and corps operations could not be mounted; subsequent fighting was conducted mostly at the brigade or battalion level. In effect, two divisions of the Indian Army, numbering 20,000, plus several thousand from the Paramilitary forces of India and the air force were deployed in the conflict zone. The total number of Indian soldiers that were involved in the military operation on the Kargil-Drass sector was thus close to 30,000. The number of infiltrators, including those providing logistical backup, has been put at approximately 5,000 at the height of the conflict. This figure includes troops from Pakistan-administered Kashmir who provided additional artillery support.

The Indian Air Force launched Operation Safed Sagar in support of the mobilisation of Indian land forces on 26 May. The Indian government cleared limited use of Air Power only on 25 May, for fear of undesirable escalation, with the fiat that IAF fighter jets were not to cross the LOC under any circumstance. This was the first time any air war was fought at such high altitudes globally, with targets at altitudes between 1,800 to 5,500 metres (6,000 to 18,000 ft) above sea level. The rarified air at these altitudes affected ballistic trajectories of air to ground weapons, such as rockets, dumb and laser guided bombs. There was no opposition at all by the Pakistani Air Force, leaving the IAF free to carry out its attacks with impunity.The total air dominance of the IAF gave the aircrew enough time to modify aiming indices and firing techniques, increasing its effectiveness during the high altitude war. Poor weather conditions and range limitations intermittently affected bomb loads and the number of airstrips that could be used, except for the Mirage 2000 fleet, which commenced operations on 30 May.

The Indian Navy also prepared to blockade the Pakistani ports (primarily the Karachi port) to cut off supply routes under Operation Talwar. The Indian Navy's western and eastern fleets joined in the North Arabian Sea and began aggressive patrols and threatened to cut Pakistan's sea trade. This exploited Pakistan's dependence on sea-based oil and trade flows. Later, then–Prime Minister of Pakistan Nawaz Sharif disclosed that Pakistan was left with just six days of fuel to sustain itself if a full-scale war had broken out.

- India attacks Pakistani positions

The terrain of Kashmir is mountainous and at high altitudes; even the best roads, such as National Highway 1 (India) (NH1) from Srinagar to Leh, are only two lanes. The rough terrain and narrow roads slowed down traffic, and the high altitude, which affected the ability of aircraft to carry loads, made control of NH 1 (the actual stretch of the highway which was under Pakistani fire) a priority for India. From their 130+ covertly occupied observation posts, the Pakistani forces had a clear line-of-sight to lay down indirect artillery fire on NH 1, inflicting heavy casualties on the Indians. This was a serious problem for the Indian Army as the highway was the main logistical and supply route. The Pakistani shelling of the arterial road threatened to cut Leh off, though an alternative road to Leh existed via Himachal Pradesh, the Leh–Manali Highway.

- Indian soldiers after winning a battle during the Kargil War

The infiltrators, apart from being equipped with small arms and grenade launchers, were also armed with mortars, artillery and anti-aircraft guns. Many posts were also heavily mined, with India later stating to have recovered more than 8,000 anti-personnel mines according to an ICBL report. Pakistan's reconnaissance was done through unmanned aerial vehicles and AN/TPQ-36 Firefinder radars supplied by the US. The initial Indian attacks were aimed at controlling the hills overlooking NH 1, with high priority being given to the stretches of the highway near the town of Kargil. The majority of posts along the LOC were adjacent to the highway, and therefore the recapture of nearly every infiltrated post increased both the territorial gains and the security of the highway. The protection of this route and the recapture of the forward posts were thus ongoing objectives throughout the war.

The Indian Army's first priority was to recapture peaks that were in the immediate vicinity of NH 1. This resulted in Indian troops first targeting the Tiger Hill and Tololing complex in Dras, which dominated the Srinagar-Leh route. This was soon followed by the Batalik-Turtok sub-sector which provided access to Siachen Glacier. Some of the peaks that were of vital strategic importance to the Pakistani defensive troops were Point 4590 and Point 5353. While 4590 was the nearest point that had a view of NH 1, point 5353 was the highest feature in the Dras sector, allowing the Pakistani troops to observe NH 1. The recapture of Point 4590 by Indian troops on 14 June was significant, notwithstanding the fact that it resulted in the Indian Army suffering the most casualties in a single battle during the conflict. Although most of the posts in the vicinity of the highway were cleared by mid-June, some parts of the highway near Drass witnessed sporadic shelling until the end of the war.

- IAF MiG-21s were used extensively in the Kargil War.

Once India regained control of the hills overlooking NH 1, the Indian Army turned to driving the invading force back across the LOC. The Battle of Tololing, amongst other assaults, slowly tilted the combat in India's favour. The Pakistani troops at Tololing were aided by Pakistani fighters from Kashmir. Some of the posts put up a stiff resistance, including Tiger Hill (Point 5140) that fell only later in the war. Indian troops found well-entrenched Pakistani soldiers at Tiger Hill, and both sides suffered heavy casualties. After a final assault on the peak in which ten Pakistani soldiers and five Indian soldiers were killed, Tiger Hill finally fell. A few of the assaults occurred atop hitherto unheard of peaks—most of them unnamed with only Point numbers to differentiate them—which witnessed fierce hand to hand combat.

As the operation was fully underway, about 250 artillery guns were brought in to clear the infiltrators in the posts that were in the line-of-sight. The Bofors FH-77B field howitzer played a vital role, with Indian gunners making maximum use of the terrain. However, its success was limited elsewhere due to the lack of space and depth to deploy it.

The Indian Air Force was tasked to act jointly with ground troops on 25 May.The code name assigned to their role was Operation Safed Sagar It was in this type of terrain that aerial attacks were used, initially with limited effectiveness. On 27 May 1999, the IAF lost a MiG-27 strike aircraft piloted by Flt. Lt. Nachiketa, which it attributed to an engine failure, and a MiG-21 fighter piloted by Sqn Ldr Ajay Ahuja which was shot down by the Pakistani army, both over Batalik sector. initially Pakistan said it shot down both jets after they crossed into its territory. According to reports, Ahuja had bailed out of his stricken plane safely but was apparently killed by his captors as his body was returned riddled with bullet wounds. One Indian Mi-8 helicopter was also lost due to Stinger SAMs. French made Mirage 2000H of the IAF were tasked to drop laser-guided bombs to destroy well-entrenched positions of the Pakistani forces and flew its first sortie on 30 May.The effects of the pinpoint non-stop bombing by the Mirage-2000, by day and by night, became evident with almost immediate effect.

In many vital points, neither artillery nor air power could dislodge the outposts manned by the Pakistani soldiers, who were out of visible range. The Indian Army mounted some direct frontal ground assaults which were slow and took a heavy toll given the steep ascent that had to be made on peaks as high as 5,500 metres (18,000 ft). Since any daylight attack would be suicidal, all the advances had to be made under the cover of darkness, escalating the risk of freezing. Accounting for the wind chill factor, the temperatures were often as low as −15 to −11 °C (5 to 12 °F) near the mountain tops. Based on military tactics, much of the costly frontal assaults by the Indians could have been avoided if the Indian Military had chosen to blockade the supply route of the opposing force, creating a siege. Such a move would have involved the Indian troops crossing the LOC as well as initiating aerial attacks on Pakistani soil, however, a manoeuvre India was not willing to exercise due to the likely expansion of the theatre of war and reduced international support for its cause.

Two months into the conflict, Indian troops had slowly retaken most of the ridges that were encroached upon by the infiltrators according to the official count, an estimated 75–80% of the intruded area and nearly all the high ground were back under Indian control.

- Washington Accord and final battles

Following the outbreak of armed fighting, Pakistan sought American help in de-escalating the conflict. Bruce Riedel, who was then an aide to President Bill Clinton, reported that US intelligence had imaged Pakistani movements of nuclear weapons to forward deployments for fear of the Kargil hostilities escalating into a wider conflict. However, President Clinton refused to intervene until Pakistan had removed all forces from the Indian side of the LOC.

Following the Washington accord of 4 July 1999, when Sharif agreed to withdraw Pakistani troops, most of the fighting came to a gradual halt, but some Pakistani forces remained in positions on the Indian side of the LoC. In addition, the United Jihad Council rejected Pakistan's plan for a climb-down, instead deciding to fight on.

The Indian army launched its final attacks in the last week of July in co-ordination with relentless attacks by the IAF, both by day and night, in their totally successful Operation Safed Sagar; as soon as the Drass subsector had been cleared of Pakistani forces, the fighting ceased on 26 July. The day has since been marked as Kargil Vijay Diwas (Kargil Victory Day) in India. In the wake of its successive military defeats in Kargil, diplomatic isolation in the international arena, its precarious economic situation, and the mounting international pressure, the Pakistani establishment was compelled to negotiate a face saving withdrawal from the residual areas on the Indian side of the LoC, thereby restoring the sanctity of the LoC, as was established in July 1972 as per the Simla Agreement.

- World opinion

Pakistan was heavily criticised by other countries for instigating the war, as its paramilitary forces and insurgents had crossed the LOC (Line of Control). Pakistan's primary diplomatic response, one of plausible deniability linking the incursion to what it officially termed as "Kashmiri freedom fighters", was in the end not successful. Veteran analysts argued that the battle was fought at heights where only seasoned troops could survive, so poorly equipped "freedom fighters" would neither have the ability nor the wherewithal to seize land and defend it. Moreover, while the army had initially denied the involvement of its troops in the intrusion, two soldiers were awarded the Nishan-E-

Haider (Pakistan's highest military honour). Another 90 soldiers were also given gallantry awards, most of them posthumously, confirming Pakistan's role in the episode. India also released taped phone conversations between the Army Chief and a senior Pakistani general where the latter is recorded saying: "the scruff of [the militants] necks is in our hands", although Pakistan dismissed it as a "total fabrication". Concurrently, Pakistan made several contradicting statements, confirming its role in Kargil, when it defended the incursions saying that the LOC itself was disputed.Pakistan also attempted to internationalise the Kashmir issue, by linking the crisis in Kargil to the larger Kashmir conflict, but such a diplomatic stance found few backers on the world stage.

As the Indian counter-attacks picked up momentum, Pakistani prime minister Nawaz Sharif flew to meet US President Bill Clinton on 4 July to obtain support from the United States. Clinton rebuked Sharif, however, and asked him to use his contacts to rein in the militants and withdraw Pakistani soldiers from Indian territory. Clinton would later reveal in his autobiography that "Sharif's moves were perplexing" since the Indian Prime Minister had travelled to Lahore to promote bilateral talks aimed at resolving the Kashmir problem and "by crossing the Line of Control, Pakistan had wrecked the [bilateral] talks". On the other hand, he applauded Indian restraint for not crossing the LOC and escalating the conflict into an all-out war.

G8 nations supported India and condemned the Pakistani violation of the LOC at the Cologne summit. The European Union also opposed Pakistan's violation of the LOC. China, a long-time ally of Pakistan, insisted on a pullout of forces to the pre-conflict positions along the LOC and settling border issues peacefully. Other organisations like the ASEAN Regional Forum too supported India's stand on the inviolability of the LOC.

Faced with growing international pressure, Sharif managed to pull back the remaining soldiers from Indian territory. The joint statement issued by Clinton and Sharif conveyed the need to respect the LOC and resume bilateral talks as the best forum to resolve all disputes.

- Pakistan

1. Two Pakistani soldiers received the Nishan-e-Haider, Pakistan's highest military gallantry award
2. Capt. Karnal Sher Khan, 27th Battalion, Sind Regiment: Nishan-e-Haider (posthumous)
3. Hav. Lalak Jan, Northern Light Infantry: Nishan-e-Haider (posthumous)

The Kargil War was significant for the impact and influence of the mass media on public opinion in both nations. Coming at a time of exploding growth in electronic journalism in India, the Kargil news stories and war footage were often telecast live on TV, and many websites provided in-depth analysis of the war. The conflict became the first "live" war in South Asia and it was given such detailed media coverage that one effect was the drumming up of jingoistic feelings.

The conflict soon turned into a news propaganda war, in which press briefings given by government officials of each nation produced conflicting claims and counterclaims. The Indian government placed a temporary News Embargo on information from Pakistan, banning the telecast of the state-run Pakistani channel PTV and blocking access to online editions of the Dawn newspaper. The Pakistani media criticised this apparent curbing of freedom of the press in India, while India media claimed it was in the interest of national security. The Indian government ran advertisements in foreign publications including The Times and The Washington Post detailing Pakistan's role in supporting extremists in Kashmir in an attempt to garner political support for its position.

As the war progressed, media coverage of the conflict was more intense in India than in Pakistan. Many Indian channels showed images from the battle zone in a style reminiscent of CNN's coverage of the Gulf War (one of the shells fired by Pakistan troops even hit a Doordarshan transmission centre in Kargil; coverage continued, however). Reasons for India's increased coverage included the greater number of privately owned electronic media in India compared to Pakistan and relatively greater transparency in the Indian media. At a seminar in Karachi, Pakistani journalists agreed that while the Indian government had taken the press and the people into its confidence, Pakistan had not.

The print media in India and abroad was largely sympathetic to the Indian cause, with editorials in newspapers based in the west and other neutral countries observing that Pakistan was largely responsible for the conflict. Some analysts believe that Indian media, which was both larger in number and more credible, may have acted as a force multiplier for the Indian military operation in Kargil and served as a morale booster. As the fighting intensified, the Pakistani version of events found little backing on the world stage. This helped India gain valuable diplomatic recognition for its position.

- WMDs and the nuclear factor

Since Pakistan and India each had weapons of mass destruction, many in the international community were concerned that if the Kargil conflict intensified, it could lead to nuclear war. Both countries had tested their nuclear capability in 1998 (India conducted its first test in 1974 while it was Pakistan's first-ever nuclear test). Many pundits believed the tests to be an indication of the escalating stakes in the scenario in South Asia. When the Kargil conflict started just a year after the nuclear tests, many nations desired to end it before it intensified.

International concerns increased when Pakistani foreign secretary Shamshad Ahmad made a statement on 31 May warning that an escalation of the limited conflict could lead Pakistan to use "any weapon" in its arsenal. This was immediately interpreted as a threat of nuclear retaliation by Pakistan in the event of an extended war, and the belief was reinforced when the leader of Pakistan's senate noted, "The purpose of developing weapons becomes meaningless if they are not used when they are needed".Many such ambiguous statements from officials of both countries were viewed as warnings of an impending nuclear crisis where the combatants would consider use of their limited nuclear arsenals in "tactical" nuclear warfare in the belief that it would not have ended in mutual assured destruction, as could have occurred in a nuclear conflict between the United States and the USSR. Some experts believe that following nuclear tests in 1998, the Pakistani military was emboldened by its nuclear deterrent to markedly increase coercion against India.

The nature of the India-Pakistan conflict took a more sinister turn when the United States received intelligence that Pakistani nuclear warheads were being moved towards the border. Bill Clinton tried to dissuade Pakistan prime minister Nawaz Sharif from nuclear brinkmanship, even threatening Pakistan of dire consequences. According to a White House official, Sharif seemed to be genuinely surprised by this supposed missile movement and responded that India was probably planning the same. In an article published in a defence journal in 2000, Sanjay Badri-Maharaj, a security expert, claimed while quoting another expert that India too had readied at least five nuclear-tipped ballistic missiles.

Sensing a deteriorating military scenario, diplomatic isolation, and the risks of a larger conventional and nuclear war, Sharif ordered the Pakistani army to vacate the Kargil heights. He later claimed in his official biography that General Pervez Musharraf had moved nuclear warheads without informing him. Recently however, Pervez Musharraf revealed in his memoirs that Pakistan's nuclear delivery system was not operational during the Kargil war something that would have put Pakistan under serious disadvantage if the conflict went nuclear.

The threat of WMD included chemical and even biological weapons. Pakistan accused India of using chemical weapons and incendiary weapons such as napalm against the Kashmiri fighters. India, on the other hand, showcased a cache of gas masks as proof that Pakistan may have been prepared to use non-conventional weapons. US official and the Organisation for the Prohibition of Chemical Weapons determined that Pakistani allegations of India using banned chemicals in its bombs were unfounded.

From the end of the war until February 2000, the Indian stock market rose by more than 30%. The next Indian national budget included major increases in military spending.

There was a surge in patriotism, with many celebrities expressing their support for the Kargil cause. Indians were angered by media reports of the death of pilot Ajay Ahuja, especially after Indian authorities reported that Ahuja had been murdered and his body mutilated by Pakistani troops. The war had produced higher than expected fatalities for the Indian military, with a sizeable percentage of them including newly commissioned officers. One month after conclusion of the Kargil War, the Atlantique Incident, in which a Pakistan Navy plane was shot down by India, briefly reignited fears of a conflict between the two countries.

After the war, the Indian government severed ties with Pakistan and increased defence preparedness. India increased its defence budget as it sought to acquire more state of the art equipment. Media reported about military procurement irregularities and criticism of intelligence agencies like Research and Analysis Wing, which failed to predict the intrusions or the identity/number of infiltrators during the war. An internal assessment report by the armed forces, published in an Indian magazine, showed several other failings, including "a sense of complacency" and being "unprepared for a conventional war" on the presumption that nuclearism would sustain peace. It also highlighted the lapses in command and control, the insufficient troop levels and the dearth of large-calibre guns like the Bofors. In 2006, retired Air Chief Marshal, A. Y. Tipnis, alleged that the Indian Army did not fully inform the government about the intrusions, adding that the army chief Ved Prakash Malik, was initially reluctant to use the full strike capability of the Indian Air Force, instead requesting only helicopter gunship support. Soon after the conflict, India also decided to complete the project, previously stalled by Pakistan, to fence the entire LOC.

The end of the Kargil conflict was followed by the 13th Indian General Elections to the Lok Sabha, which gave a decisive mandate to the National Democratic Alliance (NDA) government. It was re-elected to power in September–October 1999 with a majority of 303 seats out of 545 in the Lok Sabha. On the diplomatic front, Indo-US relations improved, as the United States appreciated Indian attempts to restrict the conflict to a limited geographic area. Relations with Israel—which had discreetly aided India with ordnance supply and matériel such as unmanned aerial vehicles, laser-guided bombs, and satellite imagery—also were bolstered.The end and victory of the Kargil War is celebrated annually in India as Kargil Vijay Diwas.

- Prime minister Vajpayee checking the guns captured from Pakistani intruders during Kargil war

Soon after the war the Atal Bihari Vajpayee government set up an inquiry into its causes and to analyse perceived Indian intelligence failures. The high-powered committee was chaired by eminent strategic affairs analyst K. Subrahmanyam and given powers to interview anyone with current or past associations with Indian security, including former Prime Ministers. The committee's final report (also referred to as the "Subrahmanyam Report") led to a large-scale restructuring of Indian Intelligence. It, however, came in for heavy criticism in the Indian media for its perceived avoidance of assigning specific responsibility for failures over detecting the Kargil intrusions. The committee was also embroiled in controversy for indicting Brigadier Surinder Singh of the Indian Army for his failure to report enemy intrusions in time, and for his subsequent conduct. Many press reports questioned or contradicted this finding and claimed that Singh had in fact issued early warnings that were ignored by senior Indian Army commanders and, ultimately, higher government functionaries.

In a departure from the norm the final report was published and made publicly available. Some chapters and all annexures, however, were deemed to contain classified information by the government and not released. K. Subrahmanyam later wrote that the annexures contained information on the development of India's nuclear weapons program and the roles played by Prime Ministers Rajiv Gandhi, P. V. Narasimha Rao and V. P. Singh.

- Pakistan

Nawaz Sharif, Prime minister at that time, after a few months a military coup d'état was initiated that ousted him and his government.

Shortly after declaring itself a nuclear weapons state, Pakistan had been humiliated diplomatically and militarily. Faced with the possibility of international isolation, the already fragile Pakistan economy was weakened further. The morale of Pakistan forces after the withdrawal declined as many units of the Northern Light Infantry suffered heavy casualties. The government refused to accept the dead bodies of many officers, an issue that provoked outrage and protests in the Northern Areas. Pakistan initially did not acknowledge many of its casualties, but Sharif later said that over 4,000 Pakistani troops were killed in the operation. Responding to this, Pervez Musharraf said, "It hurts me when an ex-premier undermines his own forces", and claimed that Indian casualties were more than that of Pakistan.The legacy of Kargil war still continues to be debated on Pakistan's news channels and television political correspondents, which Musharraf repeatedly appeared to justify.

Many in Pakistan had expected a victory over the Indian military based on Pakistani official reports on the war, but were dismayed by the turn of events and questioned the eventual retreat. The military leadership is believed to have felt let down by the prime minister's decision to withdraw the remaining fighters. However, some authors, including Musharraf's close friend and former American CENTCOM Commander General Anthony Zinni, and former Prime minister Nawaz Sharif, state that it was General Musharraf who requested Sharif to withdraw the Pakistani troops. In 2012, Musharraf's senior officer and retired major-general Abdul Majeed Malik maintained that Kargil was a "total disaster" and bitterly criticised General Musharraf. Pointing out the fact that Pakistan was in no position to fight India in that area; the Nawaz Sharif government initiated the diplomatic process by involving the US President Bill Clinton and got Pakistan out of the difficult scenario.Malik maintained that soldiers were not "Mujaheddin" but active-duty serving officers and soldiers of the Pakistan Army.

In a national security meeting with Prime minister Nawaz Sharif at the Joint Headquarters, General Musharraf became heavily involved with serious altercations with Chief of Naval Staff Admiral Fasih Bokhari who ultimately called for a court-martial against General Musharraf. With Sharif placing the onus of the Kargil attacks squarely on the army chief Pervez Musharraf, there was an atmosphere of uneasiness between the two. On 12 October 1999, General Musharraf staged a bloodless coup d'état, ousting Nawaz

Sharif.

Benazir Bhutto, an opposition leader in the parliament and former prime minister, called the Kargil War "Pakistan's greatest blunder". Many ex-officials of the military and the Inter-Services Intelligence (Pakistan's principal intelligence agency) also believed that "Kargil was a waste of time" and "could not have resulted in any advantage" on the larger issue of Kashmir. A retired Pakistan Army's Lieutenant-General Ali Kuli Khan, lambasted the war as "a disaster bigger than the East Pakistan tragedy", adding that the plan was "flawed in terms of its conception, tactical planning and execution" that ended in "sacrificing so many soldiers". The Pakistani media criticised the whole plan and the eventual climbdown from the Kargil heights since there were no gains to show for the loss of lives and it only resulted in international condemnation.

Despite calls by many, no public commission of inquiry was set up in Pakistan to investigate the people responsible for initiating the conflict. The Pakistan Muslim League (PML(N)) published a white paper in 2006, which stated that Nawaz Sharif constituted an inquiry committee that recommended a court martial for General Pervez Musharraf, but Musharraf "stole the report" after toppling the government, to save himself. The report also claims that India knew about the plan 11 months before its launch, enabling a complete victory for India on military, diplomatic and economic fronts. A statement in June 2008 by a former X Corps commander and Director-General of Military Intelligence (M.I.) that time, Lieutenant-General (retired) Jamshed Gulzar Kiani said that: "As Prime minister, Nawaz Sharif "was never briefed by the army" on the Kargil attack, reignited the demand for a probe of the episode by legal and political groups.

Though the Kargil conflict had brought the Kashmir dispute into international focus, which was one of Pakistan's aims, it had done so in negative circumstances that eroded its credibility, since the infiltration came just after a peace process between the two countries had been concluded. The sanctity of the LOC too received international recognition. President Clinton's move to ask Islamabad to withdraw hundreds of armed militants from Indian-administered Kashmir was viewed by many in Pakistan as indicative of a clear shift in US policy against Pakistan.

After the war, a few changes were made to the Pakistan armed forces. In recognition of the Northern Light Infantry's performance in the war, which even drew praise from a retired Indian Lt. General, the regiment was incorporated into the regular army. The war showed that despite a tactically sound plan that had the element of surprise, little groundwork had been done to gauge the political ramifications. And like previous unsuccessful infiltrations attempts, such as Operation Gibraltar, which sparked the 1965 war, there was little co-ordination or information sharing among the branches of the Pakistani Armed Forces. One US Intelligence study is reported to have stated that Kargil was yet another example of Pakistan's (lack of) grand strategy, repeating the follies of the previous wars. In 2013, General Musharraf's close collaborator and confidential subordinate Lieutenant General (retired) Shahid Aziz revealed to Pakistan's news televisions and electronic media, that "[Kargil] adventure' was India's intelligence failure and Pakistan's miscalculated move, the Kargil operation was known only to General Parvez Musharraf and four of his close collaborators".

- Memorial of Operation Vijay

Pakistan army losses have been difficult to determine. Pakistan confirmed that 453 soldiers were killed. The US Department of State had made an early, partial estimate of close to 700 fatalities. According to numbers stated by Nawaz Sharif there were over 4,000 fatalities. His PML (N) party in its "white paper" on the war mentioned that more than 3,000 Mujahideens, officers and soldiers were killed. Another major Pakistani political party, the Pakistan Peoples Party, also says that "thousands" of soldiers and irregulars died. Indian estimates stand at 1,042 Pakistani soldiers killed. Musharraf, in his Hindi version of his memoirs, titled "Agnipath", differs from all the estimates stating that 357 troops were killed with a further 665 wounded. Apart from General Musharraf's figure on the number of Pakistanis wounded, the number of people injured in the Pakistan camp is not yet fully known although they are at least more than 400 according to Pakistan army's website.One Indian pilot was officially captured during the fighting, while there were eight Pakistani soldiers who were captured during the fighting, and were repatriated on 13 August 1999. India gave its official casualty figures as 527 dead and 1,363 wounded.

- Kargil War Memorial, India

The Kargil War memorial, built by the Indian Army, is located in Dras, in the foothills of the Tololing Hill. The memorial, located about 5 km from the city centre across the Tiger Hill, commemorates the martyrs of the Kargil War. A poem "Pushp Kii Abhilasha" (Wish of a Flower) by Makhanlal Chaturvedi, a renowned 20th century neo-romantic Hindi poet, is inscribed on the gateway of the memorial greets visitors. The names of the soldiers who lost their lives in the War are inscribed on the Memorial Wall and can be read by visitors. A museum attached to the Kargil War Memorial, which was established to celebrate the victory of Operation Vijay, houses pictures of Indian soldiers, archives of important war documents and recordings, Pakistani war equipments and gear, and official emblems of the Army from the Kargil war.

A giant national flag, weighing 15 kg was hoisted at the Kargil war memorial on Kargil Vijay Diwas to commemorate the 13th anniversary of India's victory in the war

CHAPTER TWO

Indo-Pakistani conflicts

- **Indo-Pakistani conflicts**

Since the Partition of British India in 1947 and subsequent creation of the dominions of India and Pakistan, the two countries have been involved in a number of wars, conflicts, and military standoffs. A long-running dispute over Kashmir and cross-border terrorism have been the predominant cause of conflict between the two states, with the exception of the Indo-Pakistani War of 1971, which occurred as a direct result of hostilities stemming from the Bangladesh Liberation War in erstwhile East Pakistan (now Bangladesh).

Four nations (India, Pakistan, Dominion of Ceylon and Union of Burma) that gained independence in 1947 and 1948

The Partition of India came about in the aftermath of World War II, when both Great Britain and British India were dealing with the economic stresses caused by the war and its demobilisation. It was the intention of those who wished for a Muslim state to come from British India to have a clean partition between independent and equal "Pakistan" and "Hindustan" once independence came.Nearly one third of the Muslim population of British India remained in India.

Inter-communal violence between Hindus, Sikhs and Muslims resulted in between 200,000 and 2 million casualties leaving 14 million people displaced.Princely states in India were provided with an Instrument of Accession to accede to either India or Pakistan.

- Indian soldiers during the 1947–1948 war.

The war, also called the First Kashmir War, started in October 1947 when Pakistan feared that the Maharaja of the princely state of Kashmir and Jammu would accede to India. Following partition, princely states were left to choose whether to join India or Pakistan or to remain independent. Jammu and Kashmir, the largest of the princely states, had a majority Muslim population and significant fraction of Hindu population, all ruled by the Hindu Maharaja Hari Singh. Tribal Islamic forces with support from the army of Pakistan attacked and occupied parts of the princely state forcing the Maharaja to sign the Instrument of Accession of the princely state to the Dominion of India to receive Indian military aid. The UN Security Council passed Resolution 47 on 22 April 1948. The fronts solidified gradually along what came to be known as the Line of Control. A formal cease-fire was declared at 23:59 on the night of 1 January 1949.379 India gained control of about two-thirds of the state (Kashmir Valley, Jammu and Ladakh) whereas Pakistan gained roughly a third of Kashmir (Azad Kashmir, and Gilgit-Baltistan). The Pakistan controlled areas are collectively referred to as Pakistan administered Kashmir.

- Pakistani soldiers and tanks advance during the 1965 war

This war started following Pakistan's Operation Gibraltar, which was designed to infiltrate forces into Jammu and Kashmir to precipitate an insurgency against rule by India. India retaliated by launching a full-scale military attack on West Pakistan. The seventeen-day war caused thousands of casualties on both sides and witnessed the largest engagement of armored vehicles and the largest tank battle since World War II. The hostilities between the two countries ended after a ceasefire was declared following diplomatic intervention by the Soviet Union and USA and the subsequent issuance of the Tashkent Declaration. India had the upper hand over Pakistan when the ceasefire was declared.

This war was unique in the way that it did not involve the issue of Kashmir, but was rather precipitated by the crisis created by the political battle brewing in erstwhile East Pakistan (now Bangladesh) between Sheikh Mujibur Rahman, Leader of East Pakistan, and Yahya Khan and Zulfikar Ali Bhutto, leaders of West Pakistan. This would culminate in the declaration of Independence of Bangladesh from the state system of Pakistan. Following Operation Searchlight and the 1971 Bangladesh atrocities, about 10 million Bengalis in East Pakistan took refuge in neighbouring India. India intervened in the ongoing Bangladesh liberation movement. After a large scale pre-emptive strike by Pakistan, full-scale hostilities between the two countries commenced.

Pakistan attacked at several places along India's western border with Pakistan, but the Indian Army successfully held their positions. The Indian Army quickly responded to the Pakistan Army's movements in the west and made some initial gains, including capturing around 15,010 square kilometres (5,795 square miles) of Pakistani territory (land gained by India in Pakistani Kashmir, Pakistani Punjab and Sindh sectors but gifted it back to Pakistan in the Simla Agreement of 1972, as a gesture of goodwill). Within two weeks of intense fighting, Pakistani forces in East Pakistan surrendered to the joint command of Indian and Bangladeshi forces following which the People's Republic of Bangladesh was created. This war saw the highest number of casualties in any of the India-Pakistan conflicts, as well as the largest number of prisoners of war since the Second World War after the surrender of more than 90,000 Pakistani Army troops.In the words of one Pakistani author, "Pakistan lost half its navy, a quarter of its air force and a third of its army".

- Indo-Pakistani War of 1999

Commonly known as the Kargil War, this conflict between the two countries was mostly limited. During early 1999, Pakistani troops infiltrated across the Line of Control (LoC) and occupied Indian territory mostly in the Kargil district. India responded by launching a major military and diplomatic offensive to drive out the Pakistani infiltrators. Two months into the conflict, Indian troops had slowly retaken most of the ridges that were encroached by the infiltrators. According to official count, an estimated 75%–80% of the intruded area and nearly all high ground was back under Indian control. Fearing large-scale escalation in military conflict, the international community, led by the United States, increased diplomatic pressure on Pakistan to withdraw forces from remaining

Indian territory. Faced with the possibility of international isolation, the already fragile Pakistani economy was weakened further. The morale of Pakistani forces after the withdrawal declined as many units of the Northern Light Infantry suffered heavy casualties. The government refused to accept the dead bodies of many officers, an issue that provoked outrage and protests in the Northern Areas. Pakistan initially did not acknowledge many of its casualties, but Nawaz Sharif later said that over 4,000 Pakistani troops were killed in the operation and that Pakistan had lost the conflict. By the end of July 1999, organized hostilities in the Kargil district had ceased.The war was a major military defeat for the Pakistani Army.

- armed engagements

Apart from the aforementioned wars, there have been skirmishes between the two nations from time to time. Some have bordered on all-out war, while others were limited in scope. The countries were expected to fight each other in 1955 after warlike posturing on both sides, but full-scale war did not break out.

Insurgency in Jammu and Kashmir: An insurgency in Kashmir has been a cause for heightened tensions. India has also accused Pakistan-backed militant groups of executing several terrorist attacks across India.

Siachen conflict: In 1984, India launched Operation Meghdoot capturing all of the Siachen Glacier. Further clashes erupted in the glacial area in 1985, 1987 and 1995 as Pakistan sought, without success, to oust India from its stronghold.

Insurgency in Balochistan: An insurgency in Balochistan province of Pakistan has also caused tensions recently.

Pakistan has accused India of causing the insurgency with the help of ousted Baloch leaders, militant groups and terrorist organizations like the Balochistan Liberation Army. According to Pakistani Officials these militants are trained in neighboring Afghanistan. In 2016, Pakistan alleged that an Indian spy Kulbhushan Jadhav was arrested by Pakistani forces during a counter-intelligence operation in Balochistan.

Afghanistan conflict (1978–present): India and Pakistan had long been supporting opposing sides during the wars of Afghanistan, including during the Soviet–Afghan War and the civil wars from 1989 to 2001. In 2006, Pakistan has been accused by India for its involvement in terrorism in Afghanistan. In 2020, Pakistan accused India of trying to derail peace negotiations to end the War in Afghanistan (2001–2021).

- Past skirmishes and standoffs

Operation Desert Hawk: An operation conducted by Pakistan Armed Forces in the then disputed Rann of Kutch & Sir Creek areas in 1965. The operation ended as a success for Pakistan as it was able to regain control a significant amount of the land.

Operation Brasstacks: The largest of its kind in South Asia, it was conducted by India between November 1986 and March 1987. Pakistani mobilisation in response raised tensions and fears that it could lead to another war between the two neighbours.

2001–2002 India–Pakistan standoff: The terrorist attack on the Indian Parliament on 13 December 2001, which India blamed on the Pakistan-based terrorist organisations, Lashkar-e-Taiba and Jaish-e-Mohammed, prompted the

2001–2002 India–Pakistan standoff and brought both sides close to war.

2008 Indo-Pakistani standoff: a stand-off between the two nations following the 2008 Mumbai attacks which was defused by diplomatic efforts. Following ten coordinated shooting and bombing attacks across Mumbai, India's largest city, tensions heightened between the two countries since India claimed interrogation results alleging Pakistan's ISI supporting the attackers while Pakistan denied it. Pakistan placed its air force on alert and moved troops to the Indian border, voicing concerns about proactive movements of the Indian Army and the Indian government's possible plans to launch attacks on Pakistani soil. The tension defused in a short time and Pakistan moved its troops away from border.

2016–2018 India–Pakistan border skirmishes: On 29 September 2016, border skirmishes between India and Pakistan began following reported "surgical strikes" by India against militant launch pads across the Line of Control in Pakistani-administered Kashmir "killing a large number of terrorists". Pakistan rejected that a strike took place, stating that Indian troops had not crossed the Line of Control but had only skirmished with Pakistani troops at the border, resulting in the deaths of two Pakistani soldiers and the wounding of nine. Pakistan rejected India's reports of any other casualties. Pakistani sources reported that at least eight Indian soldiers were killed in the exchange, and one was captured.India confirmed that one of its soldiers was in Pakistani custody, but denied that it was linked to the incident or that any of its soldiers had been killed.The Indian operation was said to be in retaliation for a militant attack on the Indian army at Uri on 18 September in the Indian-administered state of Jammu and Kashmir that left

19 soldiers dead. In the succeeding days and months, India and Pakistan continued to exchange fire along the border in Kashmir, resulting in dozens of military and civilian casualties on both sides.

2019 India–Pakistan border skirmishes: On 14 February 2019, a suicide attack on convoy of India's CRPF resulted in death of at least 40 troops. The responsibility of attack was claimed by Pakistan-based Jaish-e-Mohammad. 12 days later in February 2019, Indian jets crossed international border to conduct air strikes on alleged camp of JeM in Khyber Pakhtunkhwa province of Pakistan. India claimed that it killed very large number of militants belonging to JeM. Pakistan rejected to have suffered any losses.

According to the sources and satellite imagery analysis, Indian air force appears to caused minimal damage to the buildings concerned, however, Pakistan had to close the site for one and a half month or 43 days before opened to media. The incidents escalated the tension between India and Pakistan. The following day, Indian and Pakistani air forces got locked on in an aerial engagement. Pakistan claimed to have shot down two Indian aircraft and capturing one pilot Abhinandan Varthaman. Pakistan military officials claimed that the wreckage of one Indian aircraft fell in Pakistan administered Kashmir while the other one fell in Indian administered Kashmir rumored to be a Sukhoi Su-30MKI. Meanwhile, Indian version was about loss a MiG-21 while shooting down a Pakistani F-16. The IAF also displayed remnants of an AIM-120 AMRAAM missile that they claimed could only be fired by F-16's air planes. The missiles were said to have fired against and jammed by Su-30 by IAF.

Pakistan rejected the Indian claim of an F-16 shot down. It initially released three or later on displayed all four air to air missiles of MiG-21 Bison with all missile seeker heads recovered intact from the wreckage however with mid-body of one of R-73 destroyed and claimed that non-of missiles were ever fired. Following the threats of a full-scale war, Abhinandan was released within two days. The Pentagon correspondent of Foreign Policy magazine, in a report claimed that Pakistan invited the United States to physically count its F-16 planes after the incident. Two senior U.S. defense officials told Foreign Policy that U.S. personnel recently counted Pakistan's F-16s and found none missing. A Pentagon spokesman said they was not aware of any count being conducted, but the Pentagon did not put out any official statement on the matter. However, there have been no leaks countering the Foreign Policy report. India released the electronic footage of aerial engagement to re-assert its claims. Pakistani officials has rejected radar images released by India. Stand off followed with intermittent firings across the LoC. Months later on 8 October, India on its Air Force Day, flew the same Su-30MKI "Avenger 1" aircraft in a flypast that Pakistan had claimed it had shot down during the air battle on 27 February.

2020–2021 India–Pakistan border skirmishes: The standoff intenstified when a major exchange of gunfire and shelling erupted between Indian and Pakistani troops in November 2020 along the Line of Control which left at least 22 dead, including 11 civilians. Pakistan's foreign ministry said India had violated ceasefire at least 2,729 times in 2020 which resulted in the deaths of 21 Pakistani civilians and seriously injured 206 others. In February 2021, India and Pakistan released a joint statement, stating that after discussions over established hotlines, the two sides agreed to "strict observance" of all peace and ceasefire agreements with effect from midnight of 25 February 2021. Both sides agreed existing forms of hotline contact and border flag meetings would be utilized to resolve any future misunderstanding

9 798887 836232

Printed by Libri Plureos GmbH in Hamburg, Germany